ASTERIX AT THE OLYMPIC GAMES

TEXT BY GOSCINNY

DRAWINGS BY UDERZO

TRANSLATED BY ANTHEA BELL AND DEREK HOCKRIDGE

HODDER DARGAUD
LONDON SYDNEY AUCKLAND

—Asterix at the Olympic Games—

ISBN 0 340 15591 4 (cased edition)
ISBN 0 340 19169 4 (paperbound edition)

Copyright © 1968 Dargaud Editeur
English language text copyright © 1972 Hodder & Stoughton Ltd

First published in Great Britain 1972 (cased)
Thirteenth impression 1984

First published in Great Britain 1974 (paperbound)
Eleventh impression 1984

Printed in Belgium for Hodder Dargaud Ltd,
Mill Road, Dunton Green, Sevenoaks, Kent TN13 2YJ
by Henri Proost & Cie, Turnhout

GAULISH VILLAGE

COMPENDIUM

LAUDANUM

AQUARIUM

TOTORUM

ARMORICA

BELGICA

LUTETIA

SPQR

GAUL
(ROMAN CONQUEST)
50 B.C.

CELTICA

AQUITANIA

PROVINCIA

The year is 50 BC. Gaul is entirely occupied by the Romans. Well, not entirely... One small village of indomitable Gauls still holds out against the invaders. And life is not easy for the Roman legionaries who garrison the fortified camps of Totorum, Aquarium, Laudanum and Compendium...

a few of the Gauls

Asterix, the hero of these adventures. A shrewd, cunning little warrior; all perilous missions are immediately entrusted to him. Asterix gets his superhuman strength from the magic potion brewed by the druid Getafix...

Obelix, Asterix's inseparable friend. A menhir delivery-man by trade; addicted to wild boar. Obelix is always ready to drop everything and go off on a new adventure with Asterix – so long as there's wild boar to eat, and plenty of fighting.

Getafix, the venerable village druid. Gathers mistletoe and brews magic potions. His speciality is the potion which gives the drinker superhuman strength. But Getafix also has other recipes up his sleeve...

Cacofonix, the bard. Opinion is divided as to his musical gifts. Cacofonix thinks he's a genius. Everyone else thinks he's unspeakable. But so long as he doesn't speak, let alone sing, everybody likes him...

Finally, Vitalstatistix, the chief of the tribe. Majestic, brave and hot-tempered, the old warrior is respected by his men and feared by his enemies. Vitalstatistix himself has only one fear; he is afraid the sky may fall on his head tomorrow. But as he always says, 'Tomorrow never comes.

IT IS LATE SPRING, AND EVERYTHING IS PEACEFUL IN THE LITTLE GAULISH VILLAGE WE KNOW SO WELL. OBELIX AND HIS APPRENTICE, DOGMATIX, ARE OUT DELIVERING MENHIRS, ASTERIX IS SUNBATHING OUTSIDE HIS HUT, PEOPLE LAZE ABOUT ENJOYING A SIESTA. YES, BY TOUTATIS, THE LITTLE GAULISH VILLAGE IS VERY PEACEFUL...

WHEREAS THE ROMAN CAMP OF AQUARIUM SEEMS TO BE IN A STATE OF GREAT EXCITEMENT...

BY JUPITER!

BY MERCURY!

GOOD OLD CAESAR!

GOOD OLD GLUTEUS!

YOU'LL NEVER RUN ALONE!

?

WHAT'S ALL THE NOISE ABOUT?

A MESSENGER HAS JUST COME FROM ROME WITH THE GOOD NEWS. GLUTEUS MAXIMUS HAS BEEN SELECTED TO REPRESENT ROME AT THE OLYMPIC GAMES!

GLUTEUS MAXIMUS? WHO'S HE?

YOU'RE PRETTY GREEN, AREN'T YOU, BILIUS? GLUTEUS MAXIMUS IS OUR CHAMPION! HE'S ONE OF OUR GARRISON, AND A CREDIT TO US ALL!

O GLUTEUS MAXIMUS, HOW RIGHT I WAS TO SEND YOU TO ROME FOR THE TRIALS! YOU'VE BEEN SELECTED, ALONG WITH THE BEST ATHLETES OF THE WHOLE ROMAN WORLD!

WELL, THAT'S NOT SURPRISING, O CENTURION GAIUS VERIAMBITIUS. I'M THE GREATEST!

AT AQUARIUM, WHILE THE DUTY BUCCINIST IS BLOWING 'COME TO THE COOK-HOUSE DOOR, BOYS'...

TARA TA RI!!

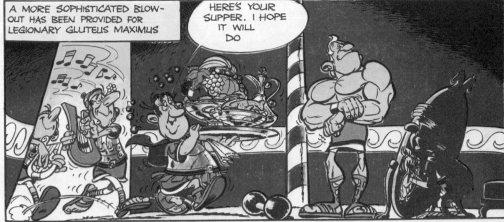

A MORE SOPHISTICATED BLOW-OUT HAS BEEN PROVIDED FOR LEGIONARY GLUTEUS MAXIMUS

HERE'S YOUR SUPPER. I HOPE IT WILL DO

NOT BAD, O CENTURION GAIUS VERIAMBITIUS. ARMY RATIONS ARE IMPROVING! WHAT ARE THESE LITTLE BLACK THINGS?

THEY'RE STURGEON'S EGGS, SENT FROM PERSIA TO OUR COMMANDING OFFICER—CAVIAR TO THE GENERAL, SO TO SPEAK!

IF YOU WIN THE GOLD PALM ·AT THE OLYMPIC GAMES THERE'LL BE EXTRA PASSES FOR THE CIRCUS AND PROMOTION ALL ROUND

SPORTING PRESTIGE IS A MATTER OF SUCH NATIONAL IMPORTANCE THAT IF YOU WIN I COULD EVEN BECOME PREFECT OF GAUL! DON'T LET ME DOWN!

STOP WORRYING— I WON'T FAIL YOU, VERIAMBITIUS

IT'LL BE A PUSHOVER. I'M THE GREATEST! NOW I'M OFF TO THE FOREST TO DO SOME TRAINING

HIS MORALE IS MARVELLOUS. WITH CONFIDENCE LIKE THAT, HE CAN'T LOSE!

FIRST A BIT OF SPRINTING — I'M THE FASTEST MAN IN THE WORLD!

MEANWHILE, IN ANOTHER PART OF THE FOREST...

I FEEL ON TOP FORM FOR A SPOT OF BOAR-HUNTING. GETAFIX GAVE ME SOME OF THE MAGIC POTION WHICH MAKES US INVINCIBLE!

I KNOW, I KNOW, AND I DIDN'T GET ANY SEEING AS I...

ONE! TWO! ONE! TWO!

???

I'M LISTENING, O ROMAN!

IT'S LIKE THIS: ONE OF MY MEN HAS BEEN SELECTED TO REPRESENT MY GARRISON AT THE OLYMPIC GAMES...

... AND SOME OF YOUR GAULS, ENTIRELY UNPROVOKED, HAVE GONE AND PUT HIM OFF HIS STRIDE!

ALL I ASK IS THAT HE SHOULD BE ALLOWED TO TRAIN IN PEACE

I'LL THINK ABOUT IT, ROMAN, AND I'LL LET YOU HAVE MY ANSWER

CHEERIO!

AVE!

THIS IS IMPORTANT! IMPEDIMENTA! MY CLOTHES! I'LL FINISH MY BATH NEXT YEAR. PUT ME DOWN, YOU TWO, AND DON'T SPILL ANYTHING!

SOON AFTERWARDS...

WHAT EXACTLY ARE THE OLYMPIC GAMES?

THE SACRED GAMES, INCLUDING TRACK AND FIELD EVENTS, ARE HELD UNDER THE AEGIS OF ZEUS. THEY TAKE PLACE EVERY FOUR YEARS, AT OLYMPIA IN GREECE, WHERE THE HELLENES LIVE, IN THE MONTH OF HECATOMBEON*

* JULY – AUGUST

THESE GAMES CONSTITUTE A SACRED TRUCE AND LAST FOR FIVE DAYS. GREAT IS THE GLORY OF THE VICTOR AND HIS PEOPLE!

CHIEF, WE'LL HAVE TO COOK SOMETHING UP!

I KNOW WHAT!

MUSHROOM SOUP!

?

15

AS THE DAY OF DEPARTURE APPROACHES, MORALE IN THE ROMAN CAMP IS GOING DOWN AND DOWN...

...WHEREAS IN THE GAULISH VILLAGE EVERYONE IS IN THE BEST OF SPIRITS. CHIEF VITALSTATISTIX IS PLANNING THE JOURNEY...

I'VE HIRED A BOAT. WE'RE GOING TO BE VERY COMFORTABLE: ONE CLASS ONLY, DECK GAMES, OPEN AIR SPORTS AND MARVELLOUS ATMOSPHERE!

THE DRUID GETAFIX HAS TAKEN CHARGE OF ALL THE ATHLETES' TECHNICAL PROBLEMS

WE MUST PLAN THEIR TRAINING CAREFULLY. FOREIGN FOOD COULD RUIN OUR CHAMPIONS' FITNESS

WE MUST HAVE A WELL-BALANCED DIET

WHAT **IS** A WELL-BALANCED DIET, O DRUID?

THAT IS!

THE BARD, CACOFONIX, IS PREPARING FOR THE POMP OF THE CEREMONIES

I WILL NOW COMPOSE AN OLYMPIC HYMN

!

CLONK!

NO, YOU ARE NOT GOING TO SING!

?
?

PAF!

WHAT'S THE MATTER WITH HIS HYMN?

I THINK HE'S SINGING FLAT

AND THE DAY BEFORE SETTING OFF, THE ATHLETES DO THEIR PACKING

18

WHAT ARE YOU MOANING ABOUT? ONE CLASS ONLY, AS AGREED. AS FOR DECK GAMES AND SPORT, YOU'RE GOING TO GET PLENTY OF THAT

AND I ADVISE YOU TO GET ROWING, FOR A START. WE MUST SAIL WITH THE TIDE

WHAT ABOUT THE ATMOSPHERE?

YOU HAVE A POINT THERE. LET THE MUSIC BEGIN!

SNAP!

BONG!

BONG!

AND DON'T MAKE ANY FUSS. YOU'RE GETTING LUXURY CLASS. ON THE USUAL CRUISES, THE PASSENGERS ARE CHAINED UP AND WHIPPED. THERE'S A LONG WAITING LIST. EVERYONE WANTS TO GET TO THE OLYMPIC GAMES!

15 A

THE GALLEY SETS OFF FOR ITS DISTANT DESTINATION, THE FASCINATING LAND OF GREECE, WITH ITS PASSENGERS IN THAT DELIGHTFUL SHIPBOARD MOOD WHICH MAKES YOU FORGET ALL YOUR WORRIES

BOM!BOM! BOM! BOM! BOM!BOM!B

THERE'S NOTHING LIKE A SEA VOYAGE TO RELAX YOU, IS THERE, ASTERIX?

NO, IT'S THE STOPS THAT ARE SO TIRING

NOW AND THEN SOME INCIDENT OR CHANCE MEETING MAKES A PLEASANT CHANGE

A PIRATE GALLEY!

WHERE?

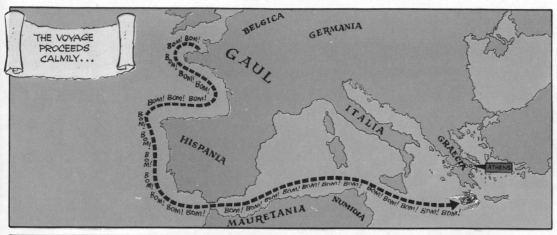

THE VOYAGE PROCEEDS CALMLY...

BOM! BOM! BOM! BOM! BOM! BOM! BOM! BOM! BOM! BOM! BOM! BOM! BOM! BOM! BOM! BOM! BOM! BOM! BOM! BOM! BOM! BOM! BOM! BOM! BOM!

BELGICA
GERMANIA
GAUL
ITALIA
HISPANIA
GRAECIA
ATHENS
MAURETANIA
NUMIDIA

...UNTIL AT LAST, ONE DAY...

WE'LL BE THERE TOMORROW, BOYS! PIRAEUS AWAITS US!

THAT'S FUNNY. I'D HAVE THOUGHT SOMEONE WOULD SAY SOMETHING, BUT I SUPPOSE IT'S ALL GREEK TO THEM

GETAFIX...

YES?

WHO IS PIRAEUS?

AH! GOOD!

PIRAEUS, AS EVERYONE KNOWS NOWADAYS, IS THE HARBOUR OF ATHENS. THE NIGHT BEFORE ARRIVING, AS USUAL, THERE IS A FAREWELL PARTY ON BOARD SHIP

♪ WHEN FATHER PAPERED THE PARTHENON... ♪

BONG!
BONG!

AND AT LAST...

21

RIGHT, BOYS! WE REPRESENT GAUL; LET US BE WORTHY OF HER! WE WON'T DRAW ATTENTION TO OURSELVES, OR MAKE FUN OF THE NATIVES, EVEN IF THEY DON'T HAVE ALL THE ADVANTAGES OF OUR GLORIOUS CULTURAL HERITAGE! ·

OFF WE GO! AND DON'T FORGET THE BOARS

HEY, ASTERIX!

WHAT IS IT?

HAVE YOU SEEN THEIR PROFILES?

SSH, OBELIX. YOU'LL PUT THEIR NOSES OUT OF JOINT!

I AM DIABETES, A GUIDE. I CAN TAKE YOU TO ATHENS BY CHARIOT AND SHOW YOU ROUND THE CITY, IF YOU LIKE

WE'VE GOT A LITTLE TIME TO SPARE BEFORE WE LEAVE FOR OLYMPIA. IT WOULD BE A PITY NOT TO VISIT ATHENS

SHALL WE GO BOYS?

YERRSS!

YOU CAN EXCHANGE YOUR SESTERTII FOR OBOLS, DRACHMAS AND MINES AT MAKALOS'S PLACE. YOU'RE QUITE SAFE; HE'S A COUSIN OF MINE

?

YOU CAN FEEL QUITE SAFE WITH THE CHARIOT DRIVER TOO. HE'S KUDOS, ANOTHER COUSIN OF MINE

JUST A MINUTE. SOMEONE'S MISSING

TEEHEEHEE!

GERIATRIX!

ALL RIGHT, ALL RIGHT! THAT'S THE TROUBLE WITH THESE ORGANIZED TRIPS, YOU'RE NEVER FREE TO DO YOUR OWN THING!

IN A CHEAP ROOM AT A SMALL ATHENS HOTEL...

FOR JUPITER'S SAKE! STOP CARRYING ON LIKE THAT!

I'VE DECIDED TO SPEND A FEW DAYS HERE IN ATHENS, SO THAT YOU CAN GET YOUR MORALE BACK BEFORE JOINING UP WITH THE OTHER ROMAN ATHLETES AT OLYMPIA...

YOU'RE RIGHT; I MUST TRY AND CALM DOWN

THAT'S IT! FORGET ABOUT THOSE GAULS!

HOORAY! WE'RE HERE, BOYS!

HELLO? WHAT'S THAT NOISE?

LET'S SEE!

!

WHAT IS IT?

MIND YOUR OWN BUSINESS! AND DON'T FORGET TO SWEEP OUT THE CORNERS!

YOU'LL BE VERY COMFORTABLE HERE, BY ZEUS. THE HOTEL IS VERY CROWDED, SO YOU'LL HAVE TO SHARE ROOMS

WHAT ABOUT THE BOARS?

YOU CAN KEEP PETS IN YOUR ROOMS. WE HAVE TO PIG IT A BIT WHEN THE PLACE IS SO FULL

OINK!

EXCEPT FOR THE BOARS, WHO ARE VERY FUSSY ANIMALS, EVERYONE IS VERY PLEASED WITH THE ACCOMMODATION

I'M WARNING YOU, I SLEEP WITH THE WINDOW CLOSED!

OINK!

COME ALONG, BOYS! DIABETES IS GOING TO SHOW US THE ACROPOLIS

AND SOON AFTERWARDS ALL OUR TRAVELLERS CAN BE SEEN ON THE SACRED ROCK OF THE ACROPOLIS, WHERE THEY ADMIRE THE PROPYLAEA, THE TEMPLE OF NIKE, AND THAT MASTERPIECE OF CLASSICAL ARCHITECTURE, THE PARTHENON...

IT REMINDS ME OF BURDIGALA...

NO, THERE'S A LITTLE SQUARE IN MASSILIA...

WHAT, NO DOLMENS?

WHAT ARE **YOU** DOING HERE?

NOT BAD, IF YOU LIKE COLUMNS

OINK!

LOOK AT THAT! LOOK AT THAT, MY FRIENDS!

SMASHING!

HOLD IT THERE!

WELL, WHAT D'YOU THINK OF IT?

MAGNIFICENT!

YES, IT'S QUITE GOOD, FOR FOREIGNERS

ATH

SPEAKING OF FOREIGNERS, HERE COME OUR FELLOW COUNTRYMEN!

25

I AM NOT YOUR FELLOW COUNTRYMAN! IF I HAD MY WAY I'D GIVE YOU BACK GAUL AND REPATRIATE EVERYBODY!

BY TOUTATIS! IT OFFENDS MY ROMAN SPIRIT TO HEAR YOU TALK LIKE THAT!

SERIOUSLY, NOW. YOU'RE NEVER GOING TO TAKE PART IN THE GAMES?

WITH THE MAGIC POTION THAT MAKES US INVINCIBLE, YOU MUST ADMIT WE'D BE STUPID NOT TO!

BUT IT'S NOT FAIR! WHAT'S GOING TO BECOME OF US?

WE'RE NOT STOPPING YOU ENTERING... IT'S JUST THAT WE'RE GOING TO WIN...

...THAT'S THE POINT!

I'M TAKING YOU TO HAVE LUNCH AT MY COUSIN'S RESTAURANT. HIS NAME'S THERMOS

THERE'S NO DEPOSIT ON THE AMPHORA. WHAT DO I DO WITH IT?

KEEP IT. IT'LL MAKE A NICE SOUVENIR

OINK!

SO OUR TOURIST FRIENDS ARE INTRODUCED TO THE JOYS OF STUFFED VINE LEAVES, KEBABS, OLIVES, WATER MELON AND RESINATED WINE.

I HAD ONE WITH ME, BUT I LEFT HIM OUTSIDE. YOU'RE NOT SUPPOSED TO BRING YOUR OWN FOOD

WHAT ON EARTH DO THEY PUT IN THEIR WINE?

OH, FOR A DROP OF AQUITANIAN WINE!

D'YOU REMEMBER THAT LITTLE RESTAURANT NEAR LUGDUNUM WHERE WE HAD THAT DELICIOUS VEAL?

IT'S NOT A PATCH ON BOAR!

OINK!

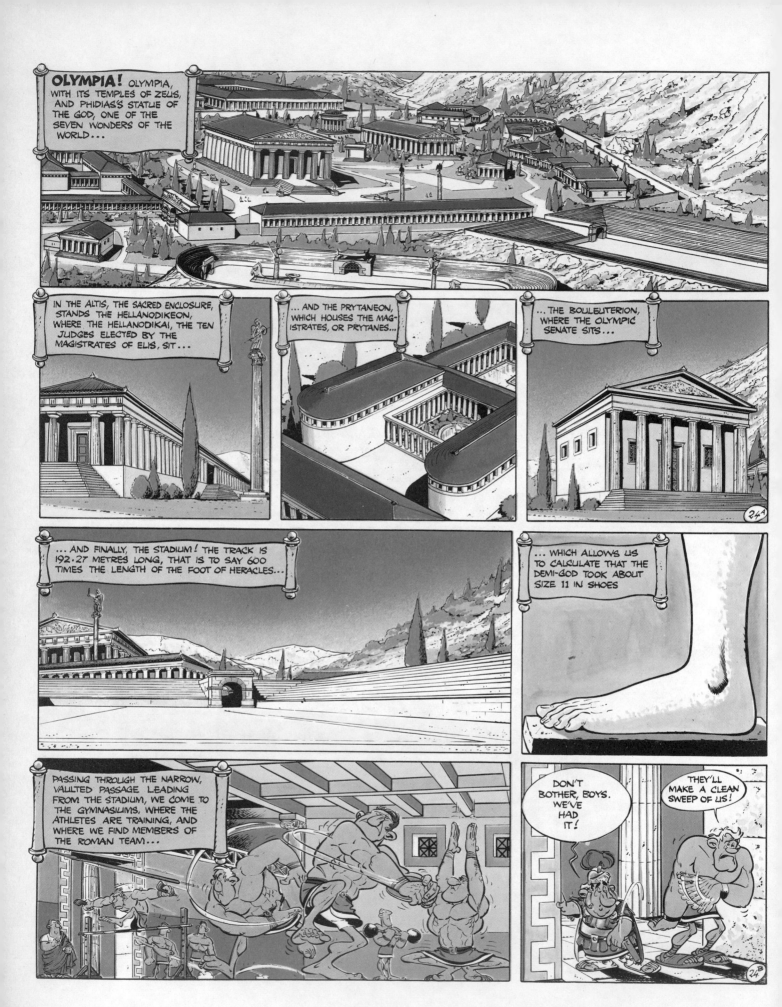

OLYMPIA! OLYMPIA, WITH ITS TEMPLES OF ZEUS, AND PHIDIAS'S STATUE OF THE GOD, ONE OF THE SEVEN WONDERS OF THE WORLD...

IN THE ALTIS, THE SACRED ENCLOSURE, STANDS THE HELLANODIKEON, WHERE THE HELLANODIKAI, THE TEN JUDGES ELECTED BY THE MAGISTRATES OF ELIS, SIT...

...AND THE PRYTANEON, WHICH HOUSES THE MAGISTRATES, OR PRYTANES...

...THE BOULEUTERION, WHERE THE OLYMPIC SENATE SITS...

...AND FINALLY, THE STADIUM! THE TRACK IS 192.27 METRES LONG, THAT IS TO SAY 600 TIMES THE LENGTH OF THE FOOT OF HERACLES...

...WHICH ALLOWS US TO CALCULATE THAT THE DEMI-GOD TOOK ABOUT SIZE 11 IN SHOES

PASSING THROUGH THE NARROW, VAULTED PASSAGE LEADING FROM THE STADIUM, WE COME TO THE GYMNASIUMS, WHERE THE ATHLETES ARE TRAINING, AND WHERE WE FIND MEMBERS OF THE ROMAN TEAM...

DON'T BOTHER, BOYS. WE'VE HAD IT!

THEY'LL MAKE A CLEAN SWEEP OF US!

28

RIGHT...ER...WELL, THE ATHLETES AND THEIR TRAINER CAN BE ADMITTED TO THE OLYMPIC VILLAGE, ALONG WITH THEIR LUGGAGE AND PROVISIONS

ARE THOSE YOUR PROVISIONS?

NO, IT'S MY LUGGAGE

UP GAULS AND AT 'EM!

WE'RE RIGHT BEHIND YOU!

UP GAUL!

HI, ROMANS!

IT'S THEM! IT'S THEM!

JUST A MOMENT! LET ME BY!

I'M PUGNATIUS! I REPRESENT ROME IN ALL THE WRESTLING EVENTS...

I HEAR YOU'RE VERY STRONG, GAUL. I DON'T BELIEVE IT! COME ON, PROVE IT, BY MINERVA!

COMING?

GLUG GLUG!

COMING!

CRACK!

CAN I PROVE IT TOO, ASTERIX?

I DON'T KNOW. ASK HIM!

CLING!

BRAOUM!

CAESAR... CAESAR REALLY IS NOT GOING TO BE PLEASED, IS HE?

HE WON'T TELL ME, ASTERIX

WHILE THE GREEK ATHLETES ARE TRAINING ENERGETICALLY, UNDER THE VIGILANT EYE OF THEIR TRAINERS, THE ALIPTES...

...THE GAULS ARE HAVING A NAP BETWEEN MEALS...

...AND THE ROMANS HAVE GIVEN UP TRYING AS WELL AS HOPE

THERE IS A TABERNA IN THE TOWN...

WHICH SURPRISES THE OLYMPIC MAGISTRATES MORE THAN SOMEWHAT

A-ROMING, A ROMING, SINCE ROMING'S BEEN MY RU-I-IN...

BY POSEIDON! THAT'S A FUNNY WAY TO TRAIN!

BY HEPHAISTOS! OUR ATHLETES WILL BEAT THESE BARBARIANS EASILY... TOO EASILY!

?!

?!

LOOK AT THAT! THEY'RE STUFFING THEMSELVES!

WHILE OUR VIRTUOUS ATHLETES ARE LIVING ON FIGS, OLIVES...

RAW MEAT AND WATER!

BUT THE GREEKS GET WIND OF SOMETHING...

SNIFF! SNIFF!

...WHICH LEADS TO REGRETTABLE INCIDENTS IN THE OLYMPIC VILLAGE

I'M NOT EATING THIS!

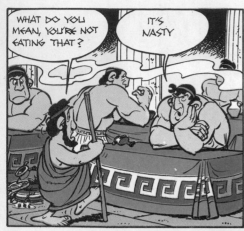

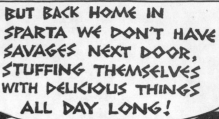

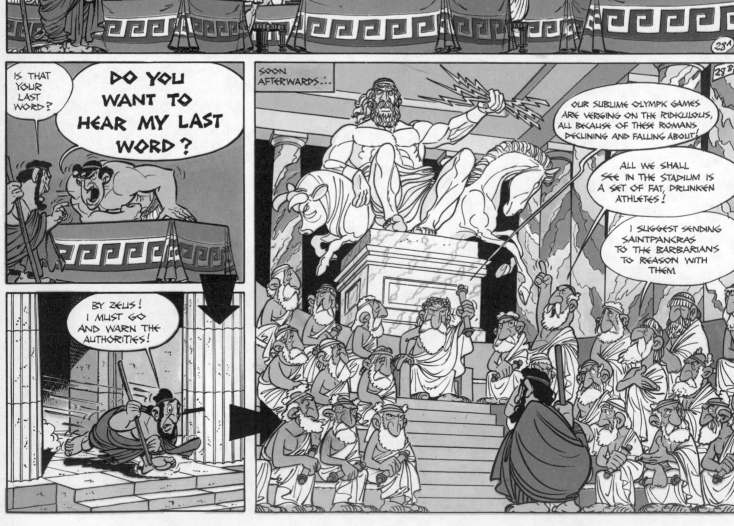

* THE BATTLE OF GERGOVIA, 52 BC

AH, HERE ARE OUR SEATS!

RIGHT! IT'S ALL SETTLED, THEN – WE ACT IN A CALM AND DIGNIFIED WAY AND RESPECT OUR OPPONENTS! WE'LL BE GOOD SPORTS AND NOT MAKE OURSELVES CONSPICUOUS

AS IF WE WOULD!

UP GAUL!

AFTER TAKING THE OLYMPIC OATH ON THE ALTAR OF ZEUS HERKIOS...

WE ARE FREE MEN OF PURE HELLENIC BLOOD WHO HAVE NEVER COMMITTED ANY CRIMINAL OR SACRILEGIOUS ACTS. WE SWEAR TO ABIDE BY THE RULES OF THE GAMES...

...THE ATHLETES ENTER THE STADIUM. THE MEN FROM THERMOPYLAE ARE THE FIRST TO PASS BY. EVERYONE IS BACK IN TRAINING; THE ATHLETES FROM MAGNESIA ARE ON A MILK DIET, THE TEAM FROM COS IS ON LETTUCE, AND EVEN THE MEN OF SALAMIS HAVE GONE VEGETARIAN...

THERMOPYLAE

...AND THERE IS A SPARTAN ASSORTMENT WHO ARE BAREFOOT. BUT A FEW OF THE ATHLETES ARE LATE; THE MARATHON TEAM HAS HAD TO COME A LONG DISTANCE, AND SOME OF THE COMPETITORS FROM ATTICA ARE MYSTERIOUSLY ELUSIVE...

SPARTA

RHODES HAS SENT ONLY ONE REPRESENTATIVE, A COLOSSUS...

RHODES

YOOHOO! BIG BROTHER IS WATCHING YOU!

SSH! LET'S BE GOOD SPORTS!

...AND IF THE ROMAN TEAM AS A WHOLE IS RECEIVED WITH GENERAL INDIFFERENCE, THE SAME CANNOT BE SAID FOR ONE OF ITS MEMBERS

GAUL! GAUL! GAUL! AS-TER-IX! AS-TER-IX! HURRAH!

GAUL

THE ATHLETES, BOTH GREEK AND ROMAN, GET INTO POSITION FOR THE FIRST RACE; 20 LAPS UP AND DOWN THE STADIUM. THEY ARE ALL, AT THE PRESENT, TENSE...

...AND THE STARTER'S MOOD IS IMPERATIVE...

GET SET! GO!

GAUL! GAUL! GAUL!

AS-TER-IX! AS-TER-IX!

GAU...L!

SPARTA

!

NOT BAD, ASTERIX

THOSE SPARTANS ARE STRONG. THE ROMANS ARE VERY FIT TOO

PFEEE!

IF YOU HADN'T MADE YOUR POTION IN A CAULDRON, I COULD HAVE ENTERED FOR THAT RACE! IF ONLY YOU'D USED AN ORDINARY POT... JUST MY LUCK!

THIS IS NOT A QUESTION OF TAKING POT LUCK *, OBELIX

* WE SEE HERE THE ORIGIN OF AN EXPRESSION WHICH HAS COME DOWN TO US FROM ANCIENT OLYMPIC TIMES

AT THE END OF THE DAY, THE ATHLETES RETURN TO THE SACRED ENCLOSURE TO TAKE STOCK...

WELL, IN VIEW OF YOUR BRILLIANT RESULTS, DO YOU THINK JULIUS CAESAR IS GOING TO BE PLEASED?

IN THE BOULEUTERION, THE OLYMPIC SENATE, THE MAGISTRATES, HELLANODIKAI, PRIESTS AND OFFICIALS HAVE ASSEMBLED. PHILIBUSTER, THE GREAT ORATOR, IS IN THE CHAIR.

NOBLE AND VENERABLE FRIENDS! OUR OWN ATHLETES ARE GOING TO WIN ALL THE PALMS, AS USUAL!

THAT'S RIGHT!

BY ATHENE!

BY APOLLO!

UP WITH US!

NONE THE LESS, IF WE DON'T GIVE THESE ROMAN BARBARIANS THE CHANCE OF WINNING ONE PALM, TOURISTS WILL TAKE NO MORE INTEREST IN OUR GAMES...

AND AS MY COUSIN DIABETES PUTS IT: NO MORE TOURISTS, NO MORE MONEY, NO MORE BUSINESS! OUR BEAUTIFUL MONUMENTS WILL FALL INTO RUIN! NO ONE WILL EVER WANT TO LOOK AT THEM THEN!

BUT WE CAN'T ASK OUR ATHLETES TO CHEAT, JUST TO LET THESE DECADENT BARBARIANS WIN!

EUREKA! I THINK I HAVE IT!

ALL ROMANS ARE SUMMONED TO THE GYMNASIUM!

THAT'S US!

I'LL NEVER GET USED TO IT!

41

ROMANS! THE OLYMPIC SENATE HAS DECIDED TO FIX AN EXTRA EVENT TOMORROW! A RACE OF XXIV STADIA, FOR ROMANS ONLY!

GOOD LUCK, AND MAY THE LEAST HOPELESS MAN WIN!

WHAT A PITY YOU CAN'T TAKE A FEW DROPS OF MAGIC POTION BEFORE THE RACE!

MAGIC POTION? YOU MEAN THE POTION IN THE CAULDRON IN THE SHED OVER THERE...?

YES, OF COURSE... I MEAN THE MAGIC POTION!

THE CAULDRON IN THE SHED OVER THERE – THE SHED WITH THE DOOR THAT DOESN'T SHUT PROPERLY?

YES, THE CAULDRON IN THE SHED OVER THERE WITH THE DOOR THAT DOESN'T SHUT PROPERLY, THE ONE THAT ISN'T GUARDED BY NIGHT... WOULD THAT BE THE ONE YOU'RE TALKING ABOUT, OBELIX?

ER... YES!

OH, BUT WE'RE NOT ALLOWED TO DRINK THE MAGIC POTION IN THE CAULDRON IN THE SHED OVER THERE...

... WITH THE DOOR THAT DOESN'T SHUT PROPERLY, THE ONE THAT ISN'T GUARDED BY NIGHT

?!

HO, HO, HO! HEE, HEE, HEE!

WHAT'S GOING ON?

OBELIX, YOU'RE BRIGHTER THAN ANY OF US!

?

YOU KNOW SOMETHING, DOGMATIX? SINCE ASTERIX AND GETAFIX TURNED ROMAN, THEY'VE BEEN CRAZY TOO!

TAP! TAP! TAP!

WOOF!

42

HERE, GLUTEUS MAXIMUS...

IF WE ARE TO BE PROMOTED, JULIUS CAESAR HAS TO BE PLEASED, AND IF JULIUS CAESAR IS TO BE PLEASED, YOU HAVE TO WIN THE RACE AND THE PALM OF VICTORY...

NOW I HAVE AN IDEA THERE MAY BE A SHED OVER THERE, WITH A DOOR WHICH DOESN'T SHUT PROPERLY, ONE THAT ISN'T GUARDED BY NIGHT, CONTAINING...

A CAULDRON OF MAGIC POTION!

SSSH!

CLAP!

RIGHT... ER... AVE, BOYS!

VERIAMBITILIS, OLD CHAP!

QUO VADIS, VERIAMBITILIS? IT WILL SOON BE DARK. WE MUST GO TO BED EARLY, WITH THE RACE TOMORROW...

OH, WE WERE JUST OFF FOR A LITTLE WALK...

JULIUS CAESAR WOULDN'T BE VERY PLEASED TO KNOW THAT WE ROMANS WEREN'T STICKING TOGETHER...

WOULD HE?

AND THAT NIGHT...

ZZZZZ ZZZZZ ZZZZZ

?

GRRRRRRRR!

HEY! DOGMATIX HAS JUST WOKEN ME UP! THERE ARE LOTS OF PEOPLE PROWLING OVER THERE, BY THE SHED WITH THE DOOR WHICH DOESN'T SHUT PROPERLY, THE ONE THAT ISN'T GUARDED BY NIGHT, CONTAINING THE CAULDRON OF MAGIC POTION . . .

DOGMATIX IS A GREAT WATCHDOG!

WELL, YOU TELL YOUR GREAT WATCHDOG TO GO BACK TO SLEEP, AND MIND YOUR OWN BUSINESS!

BUT THEY MIGHT STEAL THE CAULDRON!

THEFT OF CAULDRONS IS NOT A CRIME AMONG THE HELLENES

?!

DO YOU UNDER-STAND ANYTHING AT ALL ABOUT THE CAULDRON LAWS IN THESE PARTS, DOGMATIX?

THESE HELLENES ARE CRAZY!

COCKADOODLEDOS!

IT IS THE DAY OF THE 24 STADIA RACE, I.E. 4,614 METRES, 48 CENTIMETRES, OR AS WE MIGHT PUT IT MORE SIMPLY TODAY, 14,400 SIZE 11 SHOES LAID END TO END

ALL COMPETITORS ON THE STARTING GROOVES!

44

 proost Turnhout (Belgium)

PRINTED IN BELGIUM